TRAGEDY!
TRAGEDY!
TRAGEDY!
OH, CRUEL FATE!

Alas! We have it on good authority, that the wilderness of Cobtown has swallowed up three of our Men of Science! These gentlemen had traveled by rail-road to that remote and backward place in the hope of securing new specimens to add to their collections. The missing savants are:

CountFosco, the mineral expert who discovered the vast layer of iron pyrite that lies below our fair city. The Count came to us from Italy, where he was known as the *Reggente di Rocca*, or "King of Rocks." He was as a boulder among mere pebbles! Italy's loss was, until now, Ploomajiggy's gain. Alas! Alas!

Z. Z. Squeers, the Doctor of Desiccation and curator of the city's Museum of Animal History, is also missing. His own secret formula for the creation of animal mummies may be lost to the world forever! His Museum will be closed indefinitely.

The Ladies' Garden Circle will certainly mourn the loss of Richard Smellie, the well-known florist, should the wilds of Cobtown fail to give him up. We shall forbear all further comments about Cobtown and its hobnailed citizenry. Rather, let us offer up our expressions of admiration for our visionary men. Let us reflect upon the great loss to the world of Science. Alas! Alas!

MAGNETIC RESCUE!

Mr. Obed Spivey, Jr., has announced that the Divining Rod Society is planning a rescue mission to Cobtown in search of our missing men. We are, indeed, blessed to be living in this 19th century, when such modern scientific knowledge can be used for the benefit of all mankind.

Mr. Spivey had this to say: "We of the Divining Rod Society can track these lost men by following their unseen trail of magnetic fluxes. Our rods direct us. I must add, that if these lost gentlemen have been devoured by wild beasts, or perhaps fallen upon by the last of the mastodons, our search will prove futile."

HEDDY PEGGLER

OINKEY

LUCKY HART

JASPER PAYNE

HANS VAN RIPPER

FLIBERTY JIBBERT

EDWIN HART

PIGNAPPED!

A COBTOWN® STORY

From the Diaries of
Lucky Hart

Written by
JULIA VAN NUTT

Illustrated by
ROBERT VAN NUTT

A Doubleday Book for Young Readers

ZZ. SQUEERS

RICHARD SMELLIE

COUNT FOSCO

For
John Bartram 1699–1777
Benjamin Franklin 1706–1790
Charles Willson Peale 1741–1827
Three great Americans,
three great men of science.

J.V.N.   R.V.N.

A DOUBLEDAY BOOK FOR YOUNG READERS
Published by Random House Children's Books
a division of
Random House, Inc.
1540 Broadway
New York, New York 10036
Doubleday and the anchor with dolphin colophon are registered trademarks of
Random House, Inc.
Text copyright © 2000 by Julia Van Nutt
Illustrations copyright © 2000 by Robert Van Nutt

Cataloging-in-Publication Data is available from the Library of Congress.
ISBN: 0-385-32559-2

The text of this book is set in 15-point Greg.
Book design by Robert Van Nutt

Manufactured in the United States of America
May 2000
10 9 8 7 6 5 4 3 2 1

THE DISCOVERY

"Look what I found, Grandma!" I said as I waved a long stick with a net attached to one end. We were browsing at a neighborhood flea market.

"It looks like a butterfly net. You don't see many of those anymore. Come to think of it, you don't see near as many butterflies as you used to," Grandma said. "Maybe that's why you don't see as many of those nets."

"I think I'll start a collection of butterflies. I'm going to get this net," I told her. "I bet my friends would be impressed with all those bugs pinned down and lined up in a row."

"It's up to you," Grandma said, "but give it some thought before you start capturing wild spirits and taking their lives away just for your entertainment. When we get back home, there's something I want to show you. It's one of Grandma Lucky's diaries."

"I don't want to read about butterflies," I told her.

"I didn't say it was about butterflies, now, did I? You're going to like it. Come on, let's go back home and find it."

Back at her house Grandma headed straight up to the attic and threw open Lucky's old trunk. There on top was this story, which we read together that evening. It's quite an adventure, and sure enough, just like Grandma said, not one butterfly is mentioned.

Tuesday

Yesterday seemed like an ordinary day. I was up at Aunt Heddy's stitching my sampler. Oinkey, the wild pig who lives with her, was sitting with us. "Aunt Heddy," I asked her, "why do we call Oinkey a wild pig? He doesn't act wild."

"He is wild, Lucky," she told me. "Have you ever seen a rope around his neck to keep him here? He's wild and can walk right back into the forest if he takes a mind to. After we found him, I kept expecting him to run off. Every day I was surprised that he was still here. Something just made him choose to stay with me. We love each other now, but I don't want to forget he's got a wild heart and could run off at any time."

Just then we saw the morning train pull into the station, and three strangers got off.

Not long after, my best friend, Jasper, whose family runs Payne's Inn, ran over to Aunt Heddy's. "Three Men of Science just came to Cobtown all the way from Ploomajiggy," he said breathlessly. "They'll be staying at our inn for at least three nights. They're planning day trips way down into Mineral Gorge to seek out rare specimen to take back to their museums."

"What's rare specimen?" I asked him.

"That's just what I asked them," Jasper told me. "They said rare specimen were undiscovered animals, vegetables or minerals. According to them, Cobtown, especially Mineral Gorge, could be full of unknown specimen."

"Is that good?" I asked.

"I don't know," Jasper said. We both turned to Aunt Heddy.

She finished a stitch and said, "I've heard that some people do not believe an animal exists until they give it some fancy name and write about it in a book. These men may think this area holds some new critter that will make them famous."

"Come on, Lucky," Jasper said. "Let's get over to Ravenell's Store. The men are laying in supplies for their trip. You can take a look at them."

And that's what we did.

Mr. and Mrs. Ravenell looked busy, so we stayed out of the way, but we watched everything.

"I am Richard Smellie, head of the Ploomajiggy Society of Natural Philosophy, authority on all vegetable matter," the tiny one told the Ravenells. "These are my fellow travelers, also Men of Science. Allow me to introduce Count Fosco, recently of Italy, authority on minerals."

A big man in height and width took a silent bow.

"And this is Dr. Z. Z. Squeers, head of the Ploomajiggy Museum of Animal History," Mr. Smellie told us all.

Dr. Squeers only grunted and said, "Let's get on with it. Do you have some good sturdy rope, Ravenell? If I succeed in my search, I shall be needing it to tie down some squirming animals. They may not willingly ride the train back to Ploomajiggy. Their dim minds cannot appreciate the gift of immortality and honor that I offer them in the Museum of Animal History."

"We shall need to borrow a good map of that area," added Mr. Smellie. "You can put it with our supplies."

Well, everybody in the room laughed at that. Everybody except for the Men of Science.

"There is _no_ map of Mineral Gorge," I volunteered. "Why, nobody from around here ever goes there if they can help it. It's dark and full of sharp rocks and vines."

"No map, you say?" Count Fosco asked. "Well, I believe we three can manage to explore on our own."

They set out before lunch. That was yesterday.

They never did return to Payne's Inn, even though they had reserved rooms. Now folks are wondering just what happened to them.

That's all I know so far.

Wednesday

We had a big hailstorm here last night. It woke me up. Then I remembered the Men of Science. For two nights they have been missing and have not returned to Payne's Inn. If they are still down in Mineral Gorge, they must be suffering.

Right after breakfast I went over to Payne's Inn. Fliberty Jibbert and Old Hans Van Ripper were out front. They were talking about the missing men.

"Well, only a fool would want to go down there, anyhow," Old Hans was telling anyone who would listen.

"Were they out all night in that storm?" I asked. "I don't think they even had a tent or blanket."

"Like I said, fools, and city fools at that. Worst kind there is, know-it-alls," Old Hans said.

"Well, look here, Hans, fools or not, somebody's got to go find them," Fliberty said. "You and I know that gorge better than anybody else. We should go."

"I want to go too!" Jasper said.

"If your folks allow it, it's all right with me," Fliberty told him.

Jasper, Old Hans and Fliberty left soon after. These Men of Science, who know everything about animals, vegetables and minerals, have caused a whole lot of commotion, all in the name of science.

Thursday

Early this morning the search party found the Men of Science. Jasper came over to Aunt Heddy's to tell us all about it.

"They were right easy to find," Jasper said. "Those men were so snarled up in brambles and poison ivy that they couldn't move. They were doing a lot of hollering."

"Hans was right," Aunt Heddy said. "Those men are fools. I saw Dr. Squeers a while ago. He had swollen lumps on his head from wasp bites. Those Men of Science were so busy chasing after the unusual that they never bothered to learn about the everyday things of life. Let that be a lesson to all of us."

"I know what poison ivy looks like, Aunt Heddy," I told her.

"So do I," said Jasper.

"Well, you probably do, but what about a hickory or maple leaf?" Aunt Heddy asked.

Jasper and I looked at each other and had to admit we did not know the difference.

"We're going to start a leaf book," said Aunt Heddy. "We are going to collect all sorts of leaves that grow around here and write their names next to them. As long as I'm with you, you can't gather up any dangerous ones." She laughed. "Poison ivy is one leaf we won't be putting into our book."

"The animal man, Dr. Squeers, was angry," Jasper told us. "He kept on saying, 'I will not return empty-handed.' They are getting onto the last train back to Ploomajiggy right now."

We heard the train pull out.

"I don't think anybody in Cobtown will be sorry to see them leave," I laughed.

But I was wrong.

It all started when Aunt Heddy peeked out her back door to see if Oinkey was around. He was not.

She called for him, "Oinkey? Oinkey?" But the little wild pig did not come. Then she let loose with her "pig yodeling," which is how she calls him when he is far away. Everybody in town heard it, but Oinkey did not respond.

"Did Oinkey return to the wild, Aunt Heddy?" I asked.

"Lucky, I wish I could say that was true. Then I would not worry a bit. But there's more to this than I have told you. Let's get down to the rail-road station, quickly," she said as she headed downhill.

At the train station we ran into Fliberty. "Don't worry, Heddy," he said. "I'll help you find Oinkey."

We asked Virgil Squib, the station master, if he had seen Oinkey. "I didn't sell any train tickets to a pig, if that's what you mean," Virgil said. "I did sell three tickets to the Men of Science, who returned to Ploomajiggy on the last train. They were carrying a sizable crate labeled 'Specimen,' and sure enough, the 'specimen' was squealing and kicking."

"Oinkey was on that train! Oinkey was in that specimen crate! I have to go after him!" Heddy cried. "I have not told anyone, but this morning, before he left, that Dr. Z. Z. Squeers came to my house. He asked me to sell Oinkey to him.

"When I told him 'No!' he said, 'I don't even have to ask. You know the law. Whoever owns a pig must put the identifying notch onto the pig's ear. This pig's ears are smooth and bear no such markings. Therefore, he belongs to no one.' Squeers has claimed Oinkey as his own!" Aunt Heddy started crying.

"Calm down, Heddy," Fliberty told her. "Let's take the donkey cart and head over to Ploomajiggy. You and I will find that Museum of Animal History and that pignapper Squeers."

"That will take too much time! It's too far!" she cried.

Then Virgil spoke up. "Take the rail-road handcar. You'll be in Ploomajiggy before dawn. It's downhill most of the way."

Without a moment's hesitation they got the handcar onto the tracks. Heddy stood up front and held the lantern. Fliberty started pushing on the handles, and we watched them disappear into the dark.

I am back at my house now. At supper Papa said, "Since I am going to be in Ploomajiggy tomorrow on business, I will try to bring Aunt Heddy and Fliberty back home with me."

"What about Oinkey?" I asked.

Papa looked over at Mama and then at me. "Lucky, you come along. Maybe you can be of help. That is, if we can even find Oinkey."

That little pig must feel so alone and frightened tonight.

Poor Oinkey

Friday

This morning, Papa and I caught the first train to Ploomajiggy. When we got there Papa asked the station master if he had seen Heddy and Fliberty.

"There's no way that I could miss those two," the station master told us. "They looked windblown, and the woman had been crying. They got here before sunup and asked about the Museum of Animal History. Here's one of its handbills, if you are interested."

As we hurried up the street, I looked at the piece of paper he had handed me. It read: A SCIENTIFIC EXHIBITION OF ANIMAL MUMMIES.

"Papa, what's a mummy?" I asked.

"I'm not really sure, Lucky," he said. "But look, I have important business in town. There's Fliberty and Heddy! I will leave you with them. We'll meet up at the train station at four o'clock. Heddy! Fliberty!" he called. "Run ahead, Lucky. I will see you later."

PLOOMAJIGGY
MUSEUM
OF
ANIMAL
HISTORY

THE SQUEERS COLLECTION
A SCIENTIFIC EXHIBITION OF
ANIMAL MUMMIES
INCLUDING SERPENTS, RODENTS & POULTRY

ALL PREPARED BY Z.Z. SQUEERS,
DOCTOR OF DESICCATION, CURATOR.

I ran up to Fliberty and Aunt Heddy. They looked surprised to see me. We were standing outside the Museum of Animal History. The place was surrounded by an iron fence with spiked points. We tried the gate, but it was locked. The huge arched doors were shut. A sign out front said: MUSEUM TEMPORARILY CLOSED FOR INSTALLATION OF NEW EXHIBIT.

"If you boost me up to the ledge, I will try to get a look inside," I suggested.

That's just what I did. What I saw frightened me so much that I gasped and fell backward. I landed on the ground.

This upset Aunt Heddy even more, but I quickly told her that I was not hurt.

"What did you see in there? Was it Oinkey?" she asked breathlessly.

"No, I did not see Oinkey," I told her. "What I saw was a room full of snakes! Not ordinary snakes, either. They were funny-looking, each stretched out as straight as an arrow and holding its jaws wide open, fangs bared. They were all facing in one direction as if they all were looking at the same horrible thing!"

Fliberty and Aunt Heddy were silent for a few minutes, each trying to figure out our next move.

"Look here," I yelled as I went over the gate. "I can open it from this side." I lifted a small latch. Aunt Heddy and Fliberty joined me on the museum grounds.

The front doors were not locked, and we easily walked into the big main room. It was a frightful place, with a pointed ceiling that went way up. Everywhere we looked we saw animals unlike any we had ever seen before. They were all standing, but not moving. Some were even nailed to the wall! It was as if they had all been turned to stone.

All of a sudden I remembered the Museum of Animal History handbill. Were these frozen beasts mummies? I dared not give voice to this thought lest I frighten Aunt Heddy even more. So I kept quiet. I glanced up at Fliberty. He looked worried.

"Is this where Dr. Z. Z. Squeers lives?" I whispered to Fliberty.

"I reckon it is, Lucky, but I don't think I could sleep a wink in a place like this, how about you?" he asked, trying to smile.

"If I did I'd have bad dreams," I said. "How did all these animals come to be like this?"

Fliberty caught my eye and shook his head as if to say "Hush." I don't think he wanted Aunt Heddy to think about it too much. Maybe he didn't want <u>any</u> of us to think about it.

"We may not be able to find Oinkey in this big place," Aunt Heddy said, "but if he is anywhere nearby and he hears this, he will find us." And with that she threw back her head and let out a pig yodel.

That yodel rang out through the halls and bounced off the ceiling. Then we heard a pig squeal, a man yell and something go CRASH!

"This way!" Fliberty shouted.

We ran down a dimly lit hall to a red curtain. Fliberty threw it aside. Suddenly we were staring into a room that must have been used for creating mummies. There on a high table was Oinkey, who had partially kicked away the straps that bound him to the table. On the floor, feet up, was Dr. Squeers. He was yelling too. Oinkey had kicked him right into the mummy fluid!

"Release that pig!" Fliberty commanded.

"I will not. He is my specimen, and a rare one too," Squeers hollered.

"He is not your pig. He belongs to no one! He is his own beast, but you are correct when you say he is rare," Fliberty told him. "He is rare in the love he shares with Heddy Peggler."

"A beast is exactly what he is," Squeers shouted as he hoisted himself out of the mummy fluid. "I have given him my own scientific name, 'Squeerus porkus minor'!"

"Listen here, Squeers," Fliberty whispered as he looked him in the eye. "We will let the pig choose his fate. We are leaving. If Oinkey follows, then he has chosen to return to Cobtown. If he remains here with you, then he will have chosen to stay in Ploomajiggy as your animal mummy."

Fliberty lifted Oinkey down from the table, and we started to leave. Oinkey glared at Dr. Squeers, grunted and followed us out the door. Then Fliberty turned back and said, "Oh, and Squeers, I advise you not to follow us. You would only be exposing your, uh, self, to ridicule. It looks as if the mummy fluid has eaten a big hole right through the back of your britches!" Fliberty laughed as he led us away.

Oinkey left with us.

When we rejoined Papa for the train ride home, everybody was talking at once. Papa could hardly get the story straight at first. "What's this about snakes? Mummies? It sounds so frightful. And here I just thought you were going to get Oinkey and bring him back to Cobtown!" he exclaimed.

The train ride back home was wonderful. Aunt Heddy and I sat up front with Oinkey. I looked back at Papa and Fliberty. They were hanging on to their hats and smiling. Aunt Heddy was laughing and telling me and Oinkey about every interesting thing we passed.

"Why, I doubt if there's ever been a better day for a train ride, Aunt Heddy," I said. "And what about you, Oinkey? Are you happy to be back with us and returning to Cobtown?" I scratched behind his ears.

Oinkey turned to look up at Aunt Heddy and then at me. His little eyes twinkled, and to my surprise, he seemed to give us a smile. Yes, I'm sure that's just what I saw.

This is a true account by me,

✳ Lucky Hart ✳
1845

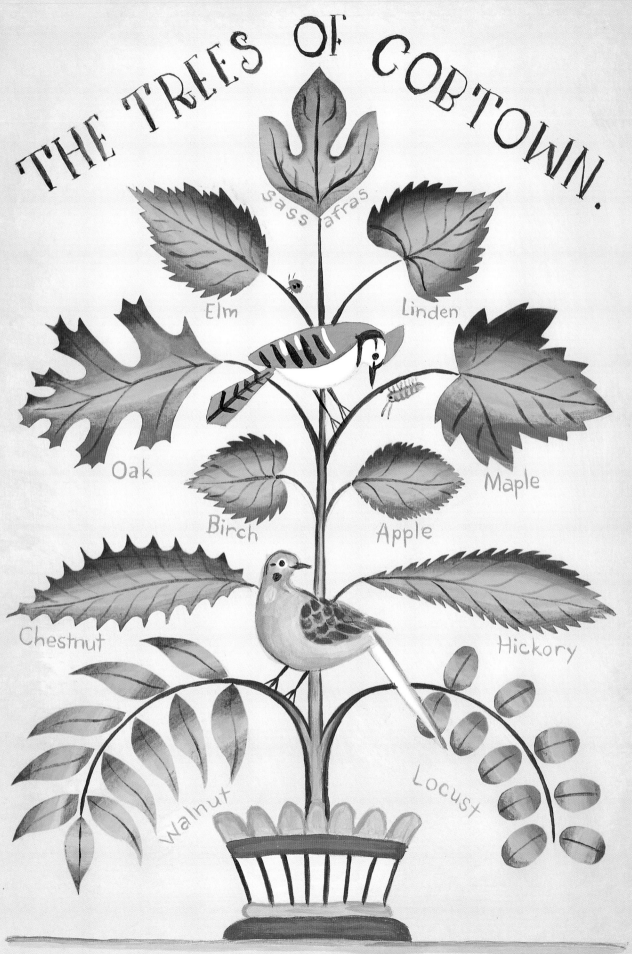

THE COBTOWN OBSERVER

I.B. HOOTIE: CHIEF CORRESPONDENT, EDITOR, PRINTER AND PUBLISHER.

MEN OF SCIENCE DISCOVER COBTOWN!

Well, neighbors, it looks like we here in Cobtown are now officially part of the civilized world! This blessing is due to the arrival of three *Men of Science* from the "Great City" of Ploomajiggy. They are here to discover and record all of our animals, vegetables and minerals, so I guess that includes us folks, too. These learned experts are: Mr. Richard Smellie, plant man; a Count Fosco, rock fancier; and **Dr. Z. Z. Squeers**, head of Ploomajiggy's Museum of Animal History. They will be staying at Payne's Inn and intend to explore Mineral Gorge.

"I have great hopes of returning to my museum with a new and rare specimen," Dr. Squeers told us.

The Men of Science.

LOST!

For two nights now, those experts from the city have not returned to their rooms at the Inn. No one has seen them, and it looks like they may have lost their way down in Mineral Gorge. ✳ ✳ ✳ ✳ ✳ ✳

SEARCH PARTY TO THE RESCUE!

Meanwhile, our own local experts, Fliberty Jibbert, Hans Van Ripper and young Jasper Payne, have set out to find the missing men. "I suspect we'll find them Ploomajiggy men pretty quick," Old Hans said, but, so far, the rescue party hasn't returned.
✳ ✳ ✳ ✳ ✳ ✳ ✳ ✳ ✳ ✳

FREAK STORM!

HAILSTONES THE SIZE OF GOOSEBERRIES

Last night Cobtown was battered by an unusually violent hail storm. Jerico Dingle tells us that the crops got kind of beat up out on his farm. "That was one powerful storm! Them big hailstones poked so many holes in my turnip greens that they look more like some fancy lace doilies than they do leaves! It did some damage, but we'll get by." ✳ Miss Lilly Fields reports that two panes of glass were broken in the school-house windows. We trust it was the storm that did the damage! The *Men of Science* were out in the heavy weather without any tents or blankets. We hope that Science didn't suffer too harshly at the hand of Nature!